The Violet Series Book 7:

Recovery

Ali Noel Vyain

This is a work of fiction. Names, characters, places, and incidents either are the product of the author's imagination or are used fictitiously. Any resemblance to actual persons, living or dead, events, or locales is entirely coincidental.

Elsewhere

eISBN: 9781005771898

print ISBN: 9798201764074

1st edition printing

alinoelvyain.wordpress.com

Also By Ali Noel Vyain

The Colonies of Earth Series
The Colonies of Earth (Eris): Different
The Colonies of Earth (Venus): In Men's Shadows
The Colonies of Earth Series: Tales From Mars
The Colonies of Earth: The Colonies Will Be Independent
The Colonies of Earth: (Orcus): The Amazons Rise Up
The Colonies of Earth (Pluto): First Time
The Colonies of Earth (Saturn & Titan): Praying for Death
The Colonies of Earth (Mercury): This Strange, Wild Land
The Colonies of Earth (The Moon): The Crossroads
The Colonies of Earth (Triton): The Mistress
The Colonies of Earth (Neptune): The Plantation Owner
The Colonies of Earth (Ceres): The Vampire's Girlfriend

The Colonies of Earth (Titania): Vampire Struggles
The Colonies of Earth (Haumea): Aftermath
The Colonies of Earth: Box Set

The Starlover Series
Book 1: Project Earth
Book 2: Uncle & Niece
Book 3: Traveling Teenager
Book 4: Cassandra the Red Tiger
The Starlover Series Box Set

The Violet Series
Book 1: A Water Nymph's Tale
Book 2: The Search for Merlin
Book 3: Retribution
Book 4: Flames & Ghosts
Book 5: The Lunatics
Book 6: Witches & Weres
Book 7: Recovery
Book 8: To Love or Not to Love
Book 9: The Joys of Working with Others
Book 10: After the Affair is Over

Book 1: A Colony of Tiny Nekos
Book 2: The Cats of Elsewhere
Book 3: Her Name is Elsewhere
Book 4: The Death of Elsewhere
Book 5: The Black Unicorn and the Winged Lion
Book 6: The Rebirth of Elsewhere
Book 7: The Childhood of Elsewhere
Book 8: The Adolescence of Elsewhere
Book 9: Elsewhere City & Spirit
The White Lion Unicorn Series Box Set

The Titanium Mysteries
Book 1: What Is She Doing Here?
Book 2: Werewolves
Book 3: Zombies
Book 4: Vampires
Book 5: For the Children
Book 6: Evil Snowpeople
Book 7: The Mortuary
Book 8: Missed Wedding
Book 9: Virtual Game
Book 10: Charm School Failure

Cyborgs
Book 1: Who is Augustus Edmunch?
Book 2: Byte Back
Book 3: The Greatest Hackers in the Universe
Cyborgs Box Set

Background Informational Books
Planets of the Universe
Dr. Butterfly's Guide to People of the Universe
The City of Elsewhere, Platinum
Modern Mordor

Cat Tale Books
Cat Tales of the Frisky9 Scarf Army
Frisky's Friends and Scarves
Cat Fairy Tales

Sir Socks Le Chat
The Life Adventures of Sir Socks Le Chat
The Diary of Sir Socks Le Chat
The Afterlife Adventures of Sir Socks Le Chat
Sir Socks Le Chat (a box set)

Poetry

Non-Fiction Books

Contents

Chapter 1 Saturn

Snowstorm was in orbit around Saturn. Antoni and Violet sat in the viewing lounge watching the planet and its moons. They were both thoughtful and wondered how this adventure was going to go. They knew they were about to meet two vampires who drank blood they bought from the local clinic.

The captain spoke through the speakers, "Attention everyone, strap yourselves in. We will be landing soon on the planet."

The computer counted down as everyone on board strapped themselves in wherever they found themselves on the ship. Violet and Antoni were no exceptions. They strapped in next to each other in the viewing lounge. They felt the ship shift as the view changed. Saturn got bigger the closer they got.

"Ready for another adventure, Violet?"

"Of course. Are you ready?"

"I'm a bit nervous to meet the vampires."

"Even though these two don't hunt? It's documented they go to the local clinic and buy blood."

Antoni sighed. "I've dealt with vampires before and it wasn't pretty either time as I'm sure you remember."

Violet blinked. "I remember. I have to admit I'm a bit nervous too."

He bit his lip. "If they try to hurt you, I could turn into animal."

"I know."

"I… I don't even know what my animal form would be. Do you have any idea?"

She shook her head.

He sighed again.

"My grandfather is still a biologist, but he doesn't know. He's not aware of many weres at all."

"Steve and Ralph live near him."

She nodded. "Steve is helping Ralph deal with being a were, but I don't know how much they know about which animal you could turn into."

He smiled at her. "You once said you thought I'd be a cat."

She smiled back. "Yes, I did. I was hoping you'd

be a cat like your dad was."

"You wish you had a cat of your own?"

They laughed.

"A cat of my own would be great. I've always liked cats and you are big enough that if we were cuddling, I wouldn't get cold."

"I see. I'll have to remember that when I'm in my animal form."

The ship landed safely at the spaceport. No one unstrapped themselves. They waited for the computer to make the announcement. The computer did several minutes later. Antoni and Violet unstrapped themselves and stood up. They left the viewing lounge to meet the captain at the airlock. Violet glowed as they walked through the corridors. Antoni smiled at her glowing and saw it didn't emanate too far from her skin and nothing around them was affected by it, except for him.

Captain Whitfield walked towards the airlock in the opposite direction of the young people. He smiled at him. "Ms. Mineur and Mr. Winchester, are you ready for your next adventure?"

"Yes," they both answered.

"Good. I hope this one will go well." The captain sighed. "I don't know about vampires. I didn't realize they were real until that first adventure of yours. Are you sure you want to talk to a couple of them?"

Antoni answered, "I'm nervous, but it's documented they buy blood from the local clinic rather than hunt anyone."

Captain Whitfield nodded. "Yes, I saw that too. I don't see how they could run a hotel and have good business if they were feeding on people."

Violet said, "Good point."

"Okay, you two can contact us if you need anything as I'm sure you know by now."

Violet motioned to her computer attached to her glasses. Antoni pulled out his communicator from his pocket.

"Very good. Now have a good adventure."

Antoni put his communicator pack into his pocket as the air lock opened. He and Violet walked out into the spaceport. They didn't say anything as they made their way out to the transport area.

"Violet, so we're not talking to the vampires here?"

"No, we'll see them on Titan. We're just here to see the Rosa Highwater Museum."

"Oh?"

"She was the original owner and founder of the Regal Highwater Titan Hotel."

"Okay."

"There should be some information on her and on Jeanine and Felix who became Ms. Highwater's inheritors."

"So, we're doing a little research before we meet them on Titan."

"Yes. I hope you don't mind."

"Not at all. I can't say I've been to many museums."

It didn't take them long to find a train to take them to the museum. They could see the dome overhead as they traveled from the spaceport to the museum. They were again quiet during the short trip. Then they found themselves right in front of the museum.

They entered and soon learned the museum was founded from Rosa Highwater's house and the house Jeanine had grown up in. They paid for their admission and were given some information about the museum and important facts. Soon Violet and Antoni were wandering around the museum and discovering what there was to learn. Violet made some notes and bookmarked the museum's website so she could refer to it later when it was time for her to write up another post on her blog.

Violet and Antoni were so busy checking out what the museum had to offer that they didn't notice Richard Williams watching them. He kept his distance from the two dear friends, but he kept a close eye on the two of them. He knew they were up to something and that it might be a good idea for him to follow and see what he could learn as to what they were up to.

It was pretty obvious to him they were up to something. It would be up to him to try and stop them from having another successful adventure. He smiled to himself. He could hear them talking.

"Antoni, have you seen enough?"

"Yeah, I think so. Are you ready to go back to the ship?"

"Yeah, I am. I know we'll have time to think about and discuss the museum as we travel to Titan."

Antoni smiled at Violet and they walked out of the museum and waited for the next train to take them back to the spaceport. Richard Williams waited with them. He needed to get to his personal transport so he could follow them to Titan. It wouldn't take long to get to Titan and check into the Regal Highwater Titan Hotel.

Richard Williams couldn't believe his luck. A plan was forming in his head. He smiled to himself as the train pulled up. They all got on board and were soon on their way back to the spaceport.

Chapter 2 An Unexpected Site

As Violet and Antoni were walking back to the *Snowstorm* they noticed a plaque in front of a leveled area. They stopped to read it. A police officer was standing by.

Antoni said, "So, this is where Jeanine's parents died?"

Violet nodded.

The police said, "Yes, her parents died here. They did their best to keep her hidden from us for years. They thought doing drugs was more important than taking care of their one child who lived."

Violet cringed.

The officer nodded. "I know it's bad. Rosa Highwater helped the young child out and kept her alive too. It was Rosa Highwater who made sure Jeanine had access to an education. Jeanine didn't care that it was virtual. She did a lot of work on her own to get a general education degree her parents tried to deny her. She also was willing to start working a regular job at a young age to support herself.

Violet smiled. "We're hoping to interview Jeanine and her co-manager Felix. We just came from the museum and learned some things."

The police office chuckled. "Not everything from their lives is in the museum, but rest assured, we'll all very proud of both Rosa Highwater and Jeanine."

Violet said, "Good. I think they both deserved the recognition."

The office nodded. "That they have."

Antoni said, "How do you feel about Felix, Jeanine's co-manager?"

The office paused for a moment. "I never knew him personally. Jeanine, Rosa Highwater and Jeanine's parents I knew fairly well. I've heard lots of good things about the young man and some bad too. I guess there will be both spoken of the same person. But as far as what I know what Felix and Jeanine did with the hotel especially after a volcano eruption, I have nothing but respect for both."

Antoni asked, "So, you would agree with how

the three are portrayed in the museum?"

"Certainly. Although, I wouldn't be surprised if there were important things missing from their lives that weren't mentioned in the museum."

Violet smiled. "I think that's usually true whenever museums are built about anything at all. It could just be the bias of the writer or creator. It's hard to avoid it no matter how hard we try to be objective."

The officer nodded. "I can well understand that. We on the police force do run into that all the time when we work on cases. We gather as much information and facts as we can. But as you know, it's still hard to avoid bias."

Violet said, "Yes, I can see how it would be hard when working on a case to avoid bias of any kind. I think when we worry about things like that it means we care about not making mistakes and wanting to get the full picture as to what is going on. It doesn't matter how hard it is, I'm willing to uncover what I can without forcing people to talk to me."

The police officer smiled. "You look familiar. I

think I've seen you before. You wouldn't happen to be Violet Nymphe Mineur who travels around the solar system and writing about her adventures she has with her best friend Antoni?"

Violet glowed. "I am."

The police office nodded to Antoni. "And you must be Antoni." He shook their hands. "It's quite an honor. I hope your next interview goes well and I look forward to your next post. As far as I can tell, you write very objectively and it makes you more credible and believable than many others who don't care to do as good as a job."

Violet said, "Thank you."

She and Antoni said their goodbyes and hurried on to the spaceport where the *Snowstorm* was waiting for them.

Chapter 3 Titan

Captain Whitfield met Violet and Antoni at the airlock. "Welcome back. Any adventure out there?"

Violet and Antoni smiled.

Violet answered, "Not really. We just went to the museum and took notes and then we found where Jeanine's parents died. We just stumbled on the second place. We found a plaque and we met a police officer who knew Jeanine, her parents and Rosa Highwater."

The captain raised an eyebrow.

Antoni said, "Yes, it was quite educational and no one bothered us this time."

Captain Whitfield laughed. "Very well. Are you ready to visit Titan?"

Antoni and Violet nodded.

Captain Whitfield pressed a button near the airlock and spoke into the microphone. "All hands prepare for takeoff."

The trio left the corridor. The captain went to the bridge. Violet and Antoni went back to the viewing lounge and strapped themselves in as soon as they had sat down. Others were running through the corridors to prepare for takeoff.

Violet and Antoni said nothing as they could hear the others getting ready. Soon the computer announced when takeoff would take place and promptly counted down to lift off. When the ship lifted off still they said nothing. They watched the stars appear in front of them once again.

Then the view shifted as the ship changed directions. Soon they were heading towards Titan. The moon became larger. Before long they could see the Regal Highwater Titan Hotel with Saturn in the background. The planet was huge and awe inspiring. It wasn't hard to figure out why Rosa Highwater had picked the location where she had put her hotel.

Antoni said nothing as he watched Violet's reaction. He smiled at her. He hoped the two vampires they were to meet and talk with would be kind. If not, then he knew he would defend Violet if things went wrong. He smiled knowing she had control over her magic and could defend herself too.

He also knew they were a good team. They had been through several adventures so far and one more wouldn't be so bad. Soon the computer was warning them of landing. They hadn't unstrapped themselves. They waited until it was safe and when the computer would make the announcement, which it made moments later.

The view was of the hotel with Saturn in the background. They were at the spaceport and they had to wait for the spaceport workers to connect a tunnel to the airlock before anyone could leave the ship.

The captain spoke through the speakers, "Attention, everyone. We have landed on Titan. As you know, this moon doesn't have a dome over the whole area. The spaceport workers are connecting a tunnel to the airlock. When they are done, we will be able to leave the ship to explore this moon. You may take shore leave and walk around and visit the Regal Highwater Titan Hotel. Please enjoy yourselves and keep your communicators with you. We may have to call you back at any time."

Cheers were heard throughout the ship. Violet and Antoni smiled and chuckled to themselves. They unstrapped themselves and stood up.

The captain continued with a smile in his voice, "Ms. Mineur and Mr. Winchester, I'll meet you at the airlock as usual."

Some time later all three met at the airlock. They smiled at each other.

"I hope your adventure will be fun and nothing scary this time. Okay?"

Violet and Antoni chuckled. Captain Whitfield joined them as did many others who were waiting to be let off the ship. The light next to the airlock changed from red to green. The captain pressed a button and the airlock opened up. He gestured to the two young adventurers. They nodded and stepped off the ship and into the tunnel. Others soon followed behind them.

They looked around them as they walked through the spaceport. Eventually, they reached a point where they were in a wide corridor. There were lots of signs directly to other tunnels which would lead to other landing places. Not all landing places were filled with spaceships. There was also a sign to let people know which way to walk to get out to the open part of Titan. It wasn't really open as there was a dome over the area.

Violet and Antoni led the way to the open part. They could see the hotel clearly once again. They could also see some other buildings nearby. It was the clinic and others necessary to the colony. The hotel was the tallest building in the area. Violet and Antoni kept walking and exploring the small town before arriving at the hotel.

Inside the hotel, Richard Williams checked in at the front desk. He smiled and went to his room. He was tired and decided to get some rest before he would explore what the hotel had to offer. Some of the crew of *Snowstorm* entered the hotel and checked in. They were ready for some relaxing and fun time off of the ship.

Violet and Antoni walked inside the hotel later on and liked what they saw when they entered the hotel lobby.

"Violet, are we going to get a room?"

"Why? The ship isn't that far away."

Antoni shrugged his shoulders. "I'll leave it up to you. I do know the hotel is reputed to have lots to do and many tourists don't leave until it's time for them to go home."

"Oh, you mean you don't want to miss the fun by having to walking between here and the ship?"

He smiled. "Yes, that's what I meant. I wasn't suggesting we share a room."

Violet chuckled. "Sure you weren't."

"You don't believe me?"

"I don't know. You've never said anything like that to me before, but things do change."

"Well, I don't think I'm ready yet."

"Don't worry about that. We have an adventure to deal with right now."

They laughed. They found information on what the hotel had to offer. They checked the screen.

"Antoni, I think it might be better if we did get a room."

"Why?"

"Then we will have unlimited access to all of this. What do you think?"

"Let's do."

They walked over to the front desk and checked into a room. They didn't say much to the attendant and soon were given a key to check out their room. They walked to the elevator and got inside. Soon they were on their way. It didn't take them long to find their room and soon they were exploring its amenities.

"Violet, have you ever worn a swimsuit before?"

"No. Have you?"

"No. These seem skimpy."

She looked at the pictures. "I think those were designed for warmer climates than we're used to."

He smiled. "At least we can buy some if we decide to get into the hot tub or pool."

"Can you swim?"

"Uh, I never tried it."

"Then we better avoid the pool. I don't want you to drown."

"Okay, then I suppose we don't need swimsuits."

"Yeah, it's wait on those. I don't know if I want to wear one of those."

"Should we try to make an appointment with Jeanine and Felix?"

Violet blinked. "I think that would be a good idea. How do we get in touch with them?"

Antoni soon found out how. They filled out a form and submitted it. "There, that's done. Are you hungry?"

"Yes. What's available?"

He searched on the room's screen and found lots of food places.

"Hmm. Can you eat any of this?"

"Uh, yes, I should be able to eat some of it."

"Are you sure?"

"Yes, I've been adding some things back into my diet and I've been okay so far."

"I don't want you to get sick."

"Okay, I'll stick with what I know I can have."

She smiled. She waited.

He smiled. "This sounds good and it meets my requirements."

"Then let's go."

They left their room moments later and walked to the little cafe. They placed their orders and soon they were enjoying a meal. There were lots of other people coming and going. Lots of talk and laughter. There were lots of other places to eat at.

Richard Williams was walking to the pool area when he saw them eating together. He smiled. His plan was coming together. They were at the hotel together. He would wait for now. It was too early to strike.

But he would strike sooner or later.

Chapter 4 You Smell Funny

Violet and Antoni walked around their floor after they had finished eating. They wanted to see what else was available. They did so many different things. They walked. They played games. They laughed. They got tired and walked back to their room. They got inside and yawned. They looked around and realized there was only one bed.

He blinked. "Uh, Violet, there's only one bed."

"I know."

"What do you suggest?"

She blinked. "I'm crawling under the covers."

"Where do you want me to sleep?"

She pulled the covers back on one side of the bed and sat down. She yawned again. She blinked and looked at the other side of the bed. It was clear there were three pillows on the bed. "This bed is huge."

He yawned again. "Is it okay if I sleep on the other side? It looks like I won't be that close to you."

"Okay." She laid back.

He walked over to the other side and pulled the covers back. He sat down and look at her. "Don't forget to take off your glasses."

"Oh, right." She sat up and took off her glasses. She set them down on the nightstand. She laid back down.

He laid down. There was enough room for another person to lay in between them.

He asked, "I wonder what my parents would think if they could see me now."

"What?" She laughed. "I bet they would want to meet me."

"I'm sure they would have liked you as would our friends back at Cat Falls."

She smiled. "I would hope so."

Their laughter faded and soon they were asleep. They were unaware there was a message sent to their room's screen. They slept unaware of much of anything except that they were sleeping in the same bed and they were alone in their room. They had a shared dream they were dancing on board the *Snowstorm*. They were alone in the ballroom as they stared deep into each other's eyes. The dream seemed to go on for a long time.

Eventually, they both opened their eyes aware of each other's breathing. They turned their heads to look at each other.

"Did you sleep well?"

She smiled at him. "We had a shared dream again."

He smiled back. "Yes, we did."

They sat up slowly. He looked in the direction of the room's screen. He saw a blinking light.

"Violet, I think we have a message."

"We do?"

He stood up. "Put your glasses on and you'll know what I'm talking about."

She chuckled and put her glasses on. He checked the screen.

"It says that Felix and Jeanine are willing to meet us in about an hour."

"Just enough time for us to take showers."

"What about clean clothes?"

"Check the 'fresher."

He checked the 'fresher in the bathroom. "Oh, they will wash and dry our clothes while we bathe. You want to go first?"

"Okay." She stood up and walked into the bathroom.

He stepped out and sat down on the bed to wait. The door slid shut. He wasn't worried about her taking too long.

She took off her glasses and her clothes. She put her clothes where she was directed and then she stepped inside the 'fresher. "Ahhh." It didn't take her long to clean up and get dried off.

She stepped out of the 'fresher to find her clothes clean and dry. She quickly got dressed and put her glasses back on. She stepped out of the bathroom moments later. "It's all yours."

He stood up and walked into the bathroom. The door slid closed behind him. He didn't take any longer than she had. Soon he was stepping out of the bathroom. "Ready?"

"Yeah. Let's go."

Violet and Antoni went in search of Jeanine and Felix. They walked to a little diner on their floor and soon saw a couple who looked rather pale. The vampires looked up when the half water nymph and part were approached their table. Both vampires made funny faces. So did the were.

Felix said, "Hello, are you Violet and Antoni?"

"Yes," answer Violet and Antoni. They sat down.

Violet smiled. "Everyone, please relax. Antoni and I are aware you are vampires. He's part were creature although he doesn't know what his animal form is. That's why you all think you smell funny."

Antoni smiled as did Felix and Jeanine.

Felix said, "I had no idea of that before. So, we just don't smell good to each other?"

Violet shook her head. "It's an age old rivalry. It might be somewhat genetic. My grandfather is a biologist and he doesn't know for sure."

Jeanine said, "So, we don't have to fight for no reason at all."

Antoni said, "Exactly."

Felix said, "Fine with me. I don't even like to

hunt. That's why I buy blood from the local clinic."

Jeanine said, "I learned to do the same from him."

Violet said, "That's comforting. So, you haven't found it a problem to be among those you could attack?"

Felix and Jeanine's eyes met momentarily. Then they looked back at their guests.

Jeanine answered, "Only once, but that was after the volcano eruption and earthquake. We were so busy cleaning up the mess that we forgot to eat at our regular time and it was nearly disastrous."

"Until a paramedic noticed what was happening to us and threw two bags of blood in our direction. We caught a bag each and drank up."

Violet and Antoni cringed.

Felix continued, "Sorry if that's gross to you. We felt better and the urge to hunt faded."

Antoni said, "I'm sure those around you were relieved too."

Jeanine and Felix nodded.

Jeanine asked, "Is that all you wanted to know?"

Violet and Antoni shook their heads.

Violet answered, "We would like to hear your side of the story about how you survived the volcano eruption and earthquake. We have done some research, but we want to hear more. We'd also like to hear about Rosa Highwater."

Jeanine smiled, "From our point of view?"

"Yes, from your point of view."

Felix said, "That could take a while. Perhaps you should order something to eat."

Antoni said, "Good idea. I think they have something here I can eat."

He and Violet placed their orders as the vampires waited and decided where to start. No one was aware of Richard Williams who was busy enjoying himself at the hotel. He found some women he could play with and decided to chase them instead of looking for Violet and Antoni for now. Perhaps it was for the best for Richard to play while he was on vacation from his job.

As Richard flirted and tested to see how far he could go without much trouble with his latest conquest, he glanced in the direction of the diner and saw Violet and Antoni receiving food and sitting with two rather pale looking people. Richard frowned at the group and turned back to the woman in question. He hoped later on he could catch the two young people and get them into serious trouble.

For now he was far too busy to deal with the young upstarts. Besides things were going exceptionally well with this woman. He wasn't about to mess this up. Richard and the woman were enjoying themselves. Why stop now? So, they soon left to have more fun together in private.

Chapter 5 Volcano

Felix asked, "How's the food?"

Both Violet and Antoni answered, "Good."

Jeanine and Felix smiled.

Felix continued. "Well, we've decided we'll talk about the volcano first. We were in bed together asleep when it erupted. It shook the whole hotel."

Jeanine said, "It was startling." She paused. "We checked out our tablets and discovered wifi got knocked out."

"So, we had to get dressed and check on others on our floor."

"We had to use the secret passageways where we found other people on the staff. They had secured their floors."

"First thing was that we had to get the wifi back up and running. The hardware is located in the office. So, we told the staff to help the wounded and we would get the wifi back up and running."

"We called for the paramedics as soon as the hotel was back online. We were cut off when the wifi was off as you any know and understand growing up not on Earth. Then we spent a long time cleaning up ruble and dealing with dead bodies."

Violet and Antoni both nodded in sync.

"That's when we lost track of time and got too hungry."

"We were lucky there was someone nearby who knew and understood what we needed."

"We had to tell employees to stop working so they could get some rest and plenty of water and food too."

"Yeah, that was interesting. Even we had to take breaks too."

Violet asked, "So, vampires need sleep too?"

Both Felix and Jeanine nodded.

Felix continued, "It took all of us a long time to clean up the hotel. Rosa Highwater must have known what she was doing when she had it built the way it was. This hotel will sway during an earthquake or volcano eruption. Structurally it will remain intact."

"Which made our job much easier. Repairs were fairly minor and casualties weren't as bad as they could have been."

"It was just a lot of work overall. Even people who were just staying in the hotel helped out too."

"Rosa's lawyer was concerned about us."

"One of the stipulations of the will was that we had to deal with something like that volcano eruption. We had to recover from it or we wouldn't own the hotel now."

Antoni asked, "Did you like the stipulations of the will?"

Felix and Jeanine shrugged their shoulders.

Felix answered, "I never really thought about it. I was too busy surviving and then I met Jeanine. I took the stipulations as an opportunity to finally prove myself. And as a way I could test and push myself to be better than I was."

Jeanine nodded. "I wasn't too surprised. I had grown up with Rosa and knew how she was. I think she set it up that way so we could feel we had earned the hotel. She probably thought both of us would do well together once we met."

Felix looked at Jeanine. "I think she knew you

better than she knew me."

"She knew me longer. I know she checked the camera footage from the hotel's cameras. So, she probably saw you working. I think she knew you by reputation and then you did speak via viewscreen."

"I was shocked when she first wanted to talk to me, but I'm glad she did. She was a much better person than my former boss."

"Neither one of us had surnames before. My parents refused me a name. Actually, I don't think they cared if I lived or died, and now I've outlived them. Part of the inheritance was that we could take her surname as our own."

"Well, we had to fulfill all the stipulations first. I'm glad she threw that one in too. I don't mind having Rosa's surname now."

"Neither do I."

"And the Rosa's lawyer is now our lawyer and lives here with his wife."

Violet and Antoni smiled.

Richard Williams was having a bit too much fun.

He couldn't keep track of all the women he was having the fun with. But he enjoyed himself so much that he forgot about Violet Mineur and Antoni Winchester for the time being. There were plenty of women in the hotel ready to have fun with him. When a few found out what he wanted and how much he wanted, they found others to join in.

He really had nothing to do for now. He knew he didn't have to go back to work for quite some time. So, he was making the most of it.

Chapter 6 Recovery Party

Violet and Antoni had finished eating. Someone stopped by and cleaned up the dirty dishes.

Violet asked, "So, after all that hard work, you decided to have a party in the whole hotel?"

Felix and Jeanine nodded. Violet raised an eyebrow.

Jeanine said, "It was quite a party."

Felix said, "It was Jeanine's idea. A good one too. We all needed to party after the horror we had been through."

"Before we were done partying and celebrating, we were live throughout the solar system. Others not just on Titan, but in other places too were partying with us and celebrating our success."

"From one extreme to another."

"We pulled ourselves and everyone else through."

"I'm so glad we did."

"So am I."

"We didn't expect the party to go on as long as it did. We weren't the only ones who needed that party."

Violet smiled. She could certainly agree that a big party such as what they had would be a great idea after the trauma they had all gone through.

Richard Williams couldn't believe his luck. He was led to a suite which had a lots of women all there for his pleasure. He smiled at each one. They weren't all dressed alike. Many posed for him. Some stood still waiting for him to make the first move. It was quite a sight. He didn't know what he had done to deserve this sort of royal treatment.

"Ladies, I am so happy to see you all."

There were oos and ahs at his statement.

"I'm not sure who I want to try out first. Any suggestions?"

Some women kept posing and showing off their best aspects. Some even starting taking off their clothes and let him watch. He approached a few naked ones and reached out to touch them.

"Hmm, yes, I think you will do for starters."

He was able to try out every woman in the room. Not always one at a time. He was euphoric that so many women were willing to please him. He didn't mind what they tried with him. He was just having way too much fun. It was a good way for him to spend his vacation from work.

He felt he had deserved this kind of attention and action. He couldn't complain right now. He was too busy enjoying himself and too many women at one time.

He was so busy with the women that he had forgotten that Violet and Antoni were still around. He gave no thought to them or what they could be possibly up to. Or why they had crossed paths once again.

Chapter 7 Thoughts on Vampires & Weres

Felix said, "Antoni, you're the only were creature I've been around. I think I'm getting used to your smell. I see no reason why we need to fight."

Antoni raised an eyebrow. "What would we fight about? Clearly, we're peaceful."

Jeanine and Violet smiled.

"Perhaps you're used to working with and among others that you don't feel the need to fight anyone."

Felix chuckled. "I was a very peaceful human. I was the one they used to pick on too much. The last bullies I had to deal with were vampires and they caused me to become one."

Antoni grimaced. "Sounds awful. How did you survive your transformation?"

"I knew what they were and so I went to the local clinic and told them what had happened. They were a bit doubtful at first until they soon learned I needed blood to survive."

"Wow."

Felix nodded. "I told them how bad I felt and

asked them to strap me down and just give me the donated blood. They listened. I think at first they were humoring me, but it helped. I was fine after a while and the blood helped. They of course recorded what was happening to me and how I reacted to them and the blood."

Jeanine said, "When the same vampires attacked me, Felix took me to the clinic and stayed with me. He was able to talk to me and help calm me down better than anyone else in the clinic could."

"I'd been through it and knew it was similar for you. So, I could tell you what it was like for me and helped you get through it."

"Yes, you did help me."

Violet asked, "Have there been any more attacks by those vampires?"

Jeanine and Felix shrugged.

Jeanine said, "We really have no idea."

Felix added, "I suppose we could ask them at the clinic. They do have information on vampires and how to identify them."

Antoni asked, "Could they have left and gone

somewhere else?"

Felix nodded. "Certainly. This is a tourist trap and they may have been tourists or vagabonds. It's hard to say." He paused. "So, what's it like to be a were creature?"

Antoni gasped. "I don't really know how to answer that. I haven't known very long that I am one."

Felix raised an eyebrow. "How did that happen?"

"My parents didn't tell me. They might have been afraid to say anything about it. I know I saw my dad as a cat. A big one and there are no cats that big on Eris. I'm sure my mother knew about it."

Felix asked, "So, the big cat was harmless?"

"Yeah, he would run around our farm, but he didn't hurt anyone. I just happen to see him a few times when I was a kid."

Felix smiled at Antoni. "Perhaps you're a big cat too."

Antoni smiled. "Violet would like that. She's fond of cats in general."

They all laughed.

Antoni went on, "As Violet knows, I have im-printed on her. It's something we weres tend to do when we met the perfect mate for us."

Felix said, "Oh, is that what you call it? Jeanine and I fell in love at first sight."

Jeanine said, "I would have to concur with that."

Felix said, "So is imprinting like falling in love?"

Antoni answered, "Perhaps something like it. Although it took me a long time to realize it had happened to me and what it meant. I just knew I wanted to be with her. But it's not quite the same. When we imprint we tend to become whatever they need us to be. In our case, I've become Vi-olet's best friend and her traveling companion."

Jeanine asked, "So, it's Violet who's driving this relationship?"

Violet chuckled. "No. It's both of us. We're just moving at the right speed which works for both of us. I didn't realize how wonderful he was at first. I just thought he was a friend. Now, I know he could be much more than that, but not until we're fully ready for that to happen."

Jeanine nodded. "I see. I guess I just didn't care after I became a vampire. I don't know how he had the self control not to come after me."

Felix smiled. "You were still human and I didn't want to hurt you. I remember you did ask me to help you to become a vampire and I refused."

Jeanine nodded. "I understand why you didn't want to change me. Then it happened from some other vampires. I'm glad you were with me to help me understand and keep me from hurting others."

Felix and Jeanine clasped hands. They looked over at Violet and Antoni.

Jeanine said, "Well, I hope when you get there completely, you both are still happy with one another."

Violet said, "I'm sure we will be."

Richard Williams laid in his hotel room by himself. He was resting after all the fun he had had. He smiled. He frowned. Violet Mineur and Antoni Winchester were still in the hotel. He sat up. He had to do something about them. They were a couple of troublemakers who had gotten in his way.

But what exactly would he do was a question he was just beginning to answer himself. He found himself thinking harder than he had before. He wasn't sure his plan was going to work out. He had a vague idea once and now he wasn't so sure. What if no one wanted to listen to him?

Then everything just clicked. He found himself contacting the women he'd have fun with lately. Many were still in the hotel. He told them what he wanted to do now. There was lots of teasing and more flirting. But it was becoming clear that he would get his revenge this time.

Chapter 8 Rosa Highwater

Jeanine said, "And now we would like to talk about Rosa Highwater. Please understand, she helped me for much of my life. Sometimes it's still a bit hard to talk about her and her kindness."

Felix nodded. "I didn't know her as long. She was already semi-retired and living on Saturn when I came to work at the hotel. But from what I knew of her and from what I learned after interacting with her, I have nothing but respect for her and her memory. I think she knew I had become a vampire and knew where I got my blood. She never gave me a hard time for it."

"She never gave me a hard time unless I called myself stupid. She would ask why I thought so and I told her it was my parents who had called me that. She then would explain they were wrong. She didn't agree with my parents' assessment of me. I think my parents just hated me and resented that I lived when all their other children had died before me."

"When Rosa first talked to me I was shocked. I wasn't expecting it at all. I wasn't a manager at the time. She admitted to me she had watched me through the cameras we have set up at this hotel. She offered me a room of my own, which was certainly not what I was expecting. She said my boss had to accept it or she would fire him as she had the power to do so.

"Then she told me about Jeanine and said she should be able to get a job at the hotel and a room of her own as well. Rosa went on to tell me to study the data she had on Jeanine and that we may end up co-managing the hotel together."

Violet said, "Wow, that's quite a compliment to both of you."

Felix nodded. "I was elated and shocked. But I'm glad she offered it to both of us. I think it would be too hard to do all by myself. I decided when she told me that I would do my best to learn. Rosa warned me that Jeanine might need to be taught some things because Rosa hadn't actually worked in the hotel for years. I didn't care at the time if I had to teach Jeanine anything. I knew I would help a new employee and see what they knew and then figure out what they needed to learn."

"My parents didn't always feed me when I was a child. Sometimes they'd forget I was living in the house. I remember not being about to stand it anymore, so I climbed out my bedroom window and ran off. I didn't know anything then. I found a door that was my height and I opened it and went inside to see Rosa Highwater sitting in her living room by herself. She asked me if I was a pixie. I told her no. She realized I was a dirty little girl and so she took me to the bathtub and cleaned me up."

Jeanine laughed. "She looked old to me with her wrinkles and gray hair. But I have to say that bath made me feel better. Then she had taken care of my clothes and made sure I had plenty after that. She also feed me that day. It was as if I had found a fairy godmother who loved me and wanted to help me out.

"But eventually, I had to go back to my parents. Rosa found out who my parents were and what they were up to. They tended to do drugs so much that it was awful. Sometimes they would have parties and pass out for quite some time. That was when I'd typically sneak out of my room by climbing out the window and went to visit Rosa. Eventually, she gave me a tablet computer and helped me sign up for school. The tablet came with headphones so I could keep quiet in my room and still get an education underneath my parents' noses.

"Not that they cared what happened to me. They were too selfish to be parents. When I became a legal adult, they forced me to move out. Rosa let me live with her. By then, I was nearly done with school and I was working a part time job to earn some money on my own.

"When I moved in, Rosa roleplayed with me that we were running a hotel. So, after she died, I wasn't surprised to learn I was to go to Titan and work at her hotel. The lawyer went and stayed in the hotel and he's still here as we already told you. He was helpful during the inheritance period when we were tested and did what we could."

Jeanine sighed. "I don't know where I would be today if Rosa Highwater didn't help me out. I don't mind that she groomed me to work in her hotel. I know she didn't have any children of her own. Perhaps Felix and I served as substitutes. I don't know for sure. She didn't strike me as a mother so much as a fairy godmother who could help me learn and grow up as I got an education and got away from my horrible parents."

Felix squeezed Jeanine's hand.

"I'm glad they're gone now. I don't miss how they treated me. I don't miss anything about them. They never took much of an interest in me and acted as if they wanted me to die. I feel I owe my life and success to Rosa Highwater."

Felix said, "You also worked for what you have. As did I. But you're right, if Rosa hadn't given us a chance, we wouldn't be in the position we are now."

Jeanine asked, "Violet, are you going to put all of what we've said onto your blog?"

"Yes. It's a great story. I do agree with Felix that you've both worked hard to get to where you are now. Rosa Highwater sounds like a wonderful person to know. I'm glad you two could tell me what she was like in her later years. It's not hard to find information on her younger years and when she started the hotel, but your information is quite unique."

Felix asked, "Did you two go to the museum on Saturn?"

Both Violet and Antoni nodded.

Felix and Jeanine shook their heads.

Felix said, "I hope you don't take all that literately. I don't agree with everything they say about us in the museum."

Violet laughed. "I'll keep that in mind. It could be a point of view and it could be that whoever came up with the museum hadn't met any of you."

Jeanine said, "We haven't met those who work at the museum and set up the exhibits."

The four young people laughed.

Antoni said, "We also found where Jeanine's parents died. There was a plaque memorializing the event and a police officer standing by who answered a few of our questions."

Jeanine rolled her eyes. "Okay, I think that's going a bit too far. What did the officer say?"

"He said he knew you, your parents, and Rosa Highwater. Oh, and he agrees with you about the museum."

There was more laughter.

Chapter 9 Labor for Twins

Bonnie grimaced. She blinked. She looked over at Clyde who was busy working on something. She couldn't think. The pain subsided. Then just as suddenly, it came back. She poked him in his ribs.

He looked up and turned his head to her. "What is it?"

"It's time."

He blinked. "Time for what?"

She narrowed her eyes as the pain was terrible once again. "Time for the twins," she said through clenched teeth.

"Oh! Right." He got up and put his tablet into his pocket. He walked over to her. "Are you ready to go?"

She nodded. He grabbed a bag they had packed of things she might need. He took her hand and they left their house. They took a little walk. Her contractions were closer together now. Every time she had one, she squeezed his hand. It wasn't hard for him to understand how bad she felt. They didn't stop until they had reached the river.

Everything was still. Bonnie and Clyde seemed to be the only people around.

"I'm ready to scream!"

Clyde looked at his wife. "Surely, they will hear you."

Soon the river moved in different ways. Bubbles formed on the surface. Some of the water towered upwards and formed into water nymphs. A water dragon surfaced.

"Ah, hello Bonnie and Clyde. I take it, it's time for the babies?"

Through clenched teeth, Bonnie answered, "Yes."

"Alright, then wade into the water. Clyde, you can stay on the bank for now. Just set the bag down."

Clyde set the bag down and helped Bonnie to step into the river. He sat down once she was low enough. They continued to hold hands. Soon a couple of water nymphs came over to help her get adjusted into a comfortable position. Herbert scanned her.

"Wow, I think your boys are ready to come out. How do you feel?"

"Like screaming."

"That's quite understandable."

"You're male. How would you know?"

"You got me there. I don't know what it feels like for you, but I do know giving birth can be painful from my studies. I certainly won't complain if you went ahead and screamed."

Bonnie breathed hard. "Fine. I'll see how I feel. I thought you said it would be better for me to give birth in the water."

"Yes, it is unless something goes wrong, but the water nymphs are here and they have experience with birthing. According to the readings you and the boys are doing fine."

"Good." Bonnie breathed hard.

Clyde encouraged her and breathed with her.

Herbert asked, "How are you, Clyde?"

"Nervous. I feel helpless."

Herbert chuckled. "I felt like that when your mother gave birth to your brother and to you.

She's fine. Don't worry about the screaming. Don't take any of it personally. She's in a lot of pain."

Clyde answered in between breaths, "Right, got it."

Bonnie screamed and floated in the river. Clyde bit his lips. The water nymphs massaged Bonnie's belly. No one paid attention to the time except for Herbert who was recording the birth. He wasn't too worried. He knew the mother and twins were still doing well. Nothing out of the unusual happened.

Eventually, a boy came out and swam to the surface. A water nymph grabbed him and held him. A few minutes later his brother swam to the surface. Another water nymph grabbed that one and held him. Then the placenta came last. The water nymphs didn't let the mother or twins to drown in the river. Eventually, a few helped Bonnie, along with Clyde's help, back onto the bank. The nymphs handed over the babies to the new parents. Each took one.

Herbert took pictures. "So, what are you going

to name them?"

Bonnie and Clyde looked at each other and at their babies.

Bonnie answered, "I'm holding Parker. He's holding Barrow."

Herbert made some notes. "Okay, and Barrow came out first. You won't have any trouble getting their birth certificates. I've got it all documented they are in the family."

Clyde smiled. "Thanks. That's one less thing for us to worry about."

Herbert smiled. "I know how it was. You'll find out soon enough. You two may not get enough sleep for a little while. You need to get to know your boys, what they need and when they need it."

Bonnie and Clyde looked at each other. She was already exhausted.

Chapter 10 Trouble Walks Over

Richard found himself surrounded by the women he had been enjoying. They were joined by some men too. All were waiting to hear about what he wanted to do to get revenge on the two young upstarts who had gotten in his way twice now. He told his story and others began to make suggestions as to what they could do to help out.

"So, where are these two people you want to prank?"

Richard smiled. "They're at the diner over there. She has red violet hair and pale blue skin. You can't miss her. Sitting next to her is her male companion."

The group turned to look. Soon they were making their way over to the young travelers. They were loud. Other people in the hotel noticed the group and weren't sure about what was going on. The group with Richard Williams in tow reached the diner. It was not a pretty sight.

"Oh, how did you get your hair that color, lady?"

Violet blinked. Antoni growled so low only she could hear him. Jeanine and Felix tensed up.

"Cat got your tongue? What are your beauty secrets? Such unusual colors for a human."

The people got closer and got into everyone's faces. They stopped asking questions. Jeanine and Felix looked at each other and nodded. They pulled out their tablets and called for security.

"Oh, are you on social media? You can't record us."

Security reached the area. An officer spoke up, "Actually, there are cameras all over the hotel. You are being recorded right now. We can build up a case against you for harassing guests and managers of the hotel."

"No way! We were just teasing! You can't do anything to us!"

"We can have you confined to your rooms until your stay is over."

"What? That is outrageous!"

Jeanine said, "Your behavior is outrageous. We expect our guests to treat everyone with respect as the staff does."

The security officer smiled. "So, if you don't calm down and stop harassing people, we will confine you to your rooms."

Everyone got quiet and slinked away. Everyone except for Richard Williams.

Violet stared at him. "Richard Williams, what are you doing now?"

"Trying to get back at you! You two keep getting in my way! You need to stop doing that!"

Violet and Antoni blinked at the same time.

Violet asked, "What are we doing?"

"Crossing my path again!"

"Really? We weren't aware that you were coming out here to this part of the solar system."

"But you got in my way on Mercury and at the University of Ceres!"

"How did we do that?"

"You took your notes and libeled me on your blog!"

Violet sighed. "I did nothing of the kind. I reported the facts. It's you who gets in the way and causes unnecessary trouble for others as you are doing right now."

"Really, you are so insulting! How dare you come here and get in my way once again!"

The security officer spoke up, "Sir, if you won't leave, I will have you confined to your room."

Richard Williams threw up his hands and turned and walked away. He griped under his breath about his recent treatment.

Antoni sighed.

Violet turned to look at him. "Are you okay, Antoni? You don't feel hot, do you?"

He shook his head. "I just wasn't sure what was going to happen."

"It's okay now. No one is threatening me or you for that matter."

Jeanine asked, "You've dealt with him before."

Felix added, "We saw it on your blog."

Violet and Antoni nodded.

Violet said, "He's a bad penny. He shows up when no one expects him and he thinks he can get better treatment from others than what he gives."

Felix said, "We know about people like that. They no longer work here."

Jeanine chuckled. "Nope, they got fired. They couldn't accept us as the co-managers."

Violet and Antoni smiled.

Chapter 11 Moving On

Jeanine asked, "So, after you write up this latest adventure, where are you headed next?"

Violet answered, "To Titania a moon of Uranus to visit more vampires."

Antoni sighed. "Are they friendly?"

Violet smiled. "Yes, they are friendly. Or at least the one I want to see is. I'm sure it will be fine. He is used to being around humans as Jeanine and Felix are."

Antoni smiled. "Okay, I think I can handle that."

Violet said, "Good."

Antoni and Violet stood up.

Jeanine and Felix stood up too.

Felix said, "I hope you've enjoyed your stay and good luck on your next adventure."

Antoni said, "I've enjoyed this in spite of the bad smell. It's good to know not all vampires are bad or dangerous."

Felix smiled. "It's good to know I don't have to worry about getting attacked by all weres I may meet."

They said their goodbyes and Antoni and Violet left the hotel. Soon they were walking across the open space under the dome back to the spaceport. They found the connecting tunnel to *Snowstorm*. They kept walking until they had crossed back through the airlock.

They didn't see the captain. Or many crew members walking around the corridor. Violet's computer beeped. She checked it.

"Oh, Bonnie just gave birth. Let me show you the pictures."

Antoni smiled at the pictures floating in front of them. "She looks exhausted."

"Well, you would be too if you had to go through labor."

They laughed.

"So, what are their names?"

"The older one is Barrow and the younger one is Parker. My grandfather is happy about it. Bonnie had a water birth and both of the babies swam to the surface on their own."

"Wow."

The galley master walked by. "Hello, Mr. Winchester and Ms. Mineur."

"Hello," they answered.

"Adorable babies. I do hope the mother is getting more sleep."

Violet and Antoni smiled.

Violet asked, "Have you seen the captain?"

"Yes, he stepped off the ship for a walk. He'll
be back, as will everyone else within 24 hours."

"Oh, right, he did grant shore leave to people."

The galley master nodded and left.

Violet put the pictures away.

"Violet, let's go to one of our rooms and then
you can work on your latest post."

"Okay, let's go to yours."

Antoni smiled and led the way to his room.
Once inside he sat down on the bed and checked
his screen for messages. There was one. It told
him when to report for duty to the galley master.
He made a note of the times when he would have
to work again. Violet sat down next to him and
checked her notes. She started writing.

Antoni watched her and he could see a projected holographic screen in front of them. He remained quiet so she could concentrate. Soon she finished her rough draft. She sighed. He raised an eyebrow at her.

"I suppose I could contact the captain to let him know where we're heading next."

"Good idea."

Violet sent the message and received one right back that they would head to Titania as soon as the rest of the crew was back on board. "Okay, that's settled."

He smiled at her.

"Now, what am I going to do with you?"

He shrugged his shoulders.

"You're no help."

"Sorry."

"No, you're not."

She hit him lightly in play. He didn't stop her. She tickled him and he laughed as his arms and legs shook uncontrollably. When he started to have trouble breathing, she stopped. She laid down next to him. He caught his breath and purred for her. They laughed. He slipped his arms around her waist.

Chapter 12 Adjustments

Herbert was busy reading his granddaughter's latest post on her site. He didn't notice the water nymphs playing around him. They of course splashed him and he wasn't responding to them as usual. They laughed and continued their play.

Just as he had finished reading, his tablet beeped with an incoming face to face call from his son.

"Hi, Clyde. Hi, Bonnie. Hi, twins."

Bonnie and Clyde grunted. It was clear they both had dark circles underneath their eyes.

"Having a little trouble?"

The parents nodded.

"Ah, how bad is it?"

Bonnie answered, "I've had a bit of trouble feeding them and so we got some formula too."

Clyde answered, "And it seems to be helping, but these boys get hungry sometimes in the night."

Herbert nodded. "Yes, I remember. They should grow out of it. Any other trouble?"

Bonnie said, "They don't want to sleep at night."

Herbert sighed. "That's a tough one. I don't know if they will ever grow out of that. Anything else?"

Clyde answered, "Just a little trouble changing their diapers. They were spraying us, but I think we got that to stop now."

Herbert nodded. "That can be hard to learn with boys. Sooner or later they learn control and they stop doing it or do it on purpose."

Both parents sighed.

"Hey, both of you are still alive and the babies are fine. It's always hard in the beginning. I remember. It turned my world upside down. Relax, Clyde, it was in a good way. Similar to how your mother turned my world upside down."

Clyde said, "Sometimes I still miss her. I don't know how you can take it."

Herbert sighed. "I miss her terribly. I wish she hadn't died, but there wasn't anything I could do. It was too late when we found out. At least she went peacefully in the end."

Clyde sighed.

"Have you read the latest from our dear Violet?"

Clyde said, "We haven't had time. Please fill us in."

"She and Antoni are doing well. Apparently Richard Williams crossed their path again and was threatened with a lockdown in his hotel room."

Bonnie said, "Ugh. He's terrible."

Herbert nodded and continued, "This time they talked to two vampires who agreed that Antoni didn't smell good to them. Antoni agreed they didn't smell good to him either. There was no fighting as all are peaceful. Apparently from what Steve tells me, it's the same for him. He thinks vampires smell bad. He uses caution whenever he comes across one."

Bonnie nodded. "Violet is a very brave woman. I don't think we need to worry about her, but sometimes I still do."

Herbert chuckled. "It's hard not to worry when you care. I still worried too, but she has enough of

Dory in her that I know she will be alright. She's survived some pretty bad adventures so far and yet she and Antoni are still together and happy."

The parents smiled and found their twins were fast asleep in their arms. They wondered what kinds of adventures their identical twins would discover once they were old enough.